FRIENDS TO THE RESCUE

DORIS ORGEL
Illustrated by BOB DORSEY

Bank Street

Hyperion Paperbacks for Children
New York

For Jennifer Kemp
—D. O.

First Hyperion Paperback edition 1996
Text ©1996 by Doris Orgel.
Illustrations ©1996 by Bob Dorsey.
Printed in the United States of America.
1 3 5 7 9 10 8 6 4 2
The text for this book is set in 12-point Berling Roman.

Library of Congress Cataloging-in-Publication Data

Orgel, Doris.
    Friends to the rescue / Doris Orgel ; illustrated by Bob Dorsey. — 1st
Hyperion Paperbacks ed.
        p.   cm. — (The West Side kids ; #3)
    Summary: Katie is unhappy after she and he mother move in with
her very proper grandmother, until she makes friends with Luz
Mendes, who makes her feel welcome and teaches her how to
rollerblade.
    ISBN 0-7868-2087-X (lib. bdg.) — ISBN 0-7868-1045-9 (pbk.)
    [1. Friendship—Fiction. 2. City and town life—Fiction. 3. Moving, Household—
Fiction.] I. Dorsey, Bob, ill. II. Title. III. Series: West Side kids ; 3.
PZ7.0632Un   1996
[Fic]—dc20
95-33605

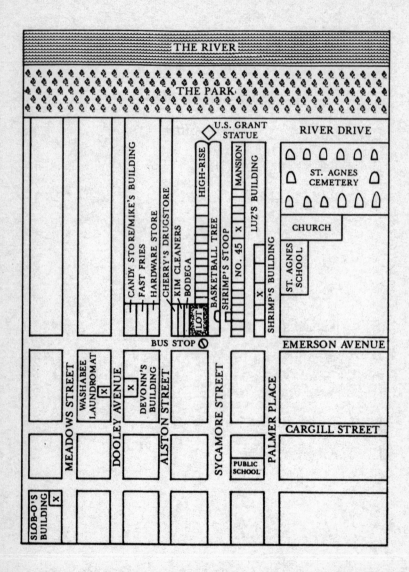

CONTENTS

# **1** NOT LIKE HOME

"KATHERINE, DON'T SLUMP," said my grandmother. "Stand up straight." She poked me in the back—ouch!

Why does she have to be like that?

It was hot and sticky out. We were walking home from the grocery store. I had "slumped" because I was watching little bits of stone in the sidewalk catch the sun and gleam.

Oh—did I say "home"? I take it back. Grandmother's place does *not* feel like home.

Home is where we lived before, just me and Mom. But Mom lost her job and we ran out of rent money. So we had to move in with *her.*

Grandmother has a huge apartment. It's in the only fancy high-rise building on this block of Sycamore Street. Mom and I have our own rooms. Mine has a thick blue rug on the floor. Over the bed there's a dark blue canopy. When I lie on my back and look up, it's like having my own private sky.

But I still don't like it here.

I *do* like the sidewalk on this street, a lot. I like how it sparkles and how wide it is. It's almost as smooth as the floor of a gym.

Perfect for blading, I thought. Just then a girl about

my age whizzed past—on Rollerblades.

The wind whipped her curly hair all around. She moved her arms back and forth in rhythm with her fast glides. She looked great. I bet she was feeling wonderful. I could just imagine how I'd feel.

I wanted to be her *so* bad! Or at least be able to skate like that.

"Tsk, tsk, a dangerous sport," said Grandmother. "Someone should inform that child that sidewalks are intended for walking."

By then we were at Number 45, Grandmother's building.

The doorman said, "Hello, Ms. Davidson. Hi, kid."

Grandmother greeted him back: "Hello, Felipe." And she told him in a scolding voice, "The 'kid' has a name: It's Katherine."

"Katie," I said under my breath. "Katherine" sounds like a lady in an evening gown with high-heeled shoes and maybe a fur coat.

Grandmother pushed the button for the elevator.

I asked, "Can I wait down here for Mom?"

"*May* I. No." She shook her head. "No" is Grandmother's favorite word.

"Just for a little while? Mom said she'd be back around now. Please, Grandmother, *may* I?"

"Well, all right. Just for a few minutes. But don't bother Felipe. He has to pay full attention to his job."

The elevator came and she marched in.

- -

* * *

I said, "I won't bother you, Felipe. But can I ask you
something?"

"Sure."

"Is it okay if I call you Pony?"

I'd heard other kids in the building and on the block
call him that. On account of his ponytail. It looks kind
of weird with the uniform he has to wear—brown
with gold braid on the shoulders and down the sides of
the pants. But even so, that ponytail looks good on
him.

Pony said, "Fine with me. Just not in front of your
grandma. She wouldn't approve."

"My grand*mother*," I said. "She doesn't approve of
'grandma,' either."

He laughed. "That figures. Sit down, kid."

The doormen in this building have to stand next to
the intercom and be ready to answer it. Next to the
intercom there's a bench. It had a newspaper on it.

I sat down. I asked, "Can I borrow your paper for a
second?"

"Sure. Look at it all you want, Katherine."

"Katie," I said. "That's what my friends call me." At
least they did when I still had friends, back where we
used to live.

I turned to the real estate pages and looked at apartment ads.

"Thinking of moving out already?" asked Pony. "You

-- -- -- -- -- -- -- -- -- -- -- -- -- -- -- -- --

just moved in a week ago. Don't you like it here?"

"Not too much."

Then we got to talking. He asked me where I lived before. I told him about our old neighborhood. The kids I hung out with. The fun we had. How Mom and me got along just great with nobody to boss us around. . . .

I stopped there. I didn't want to sound ungrateful.

"Yeah," said Pony. "But you know something, Katie? It can't be easy for Ms. Davidson, either. She's been living on her own for I don't know how many years. She's not used to being a grandma—oops, grandmother."

"You're right," I said. And I thought to myself, She sure has a lot to learn.

Then I looked out the front door and saw Mom coming down the block.

"Thanks for the paper, Pony!"

I gave it back and dashed outside.

My mom has brown hair, short and straight, and green eyes just like mine. She's built like me, too—thin and bouncy. She's the kind of grown-up who still knows how to skip. Sometimes she'll go skipping down a street and not think a thing of it.

But now she trudged along slowly, carrying her big, heavy portfolio with her art samples in it. She was "slumping," as Grandmother would say.

Mom had gone to an interview for a job designing

wallpaper. I could see by the look on her face that it didn't go well.

I said, "Too bad for that wallpaper place. They must need glasses, or they'd see what a good artist you are." And I hugged her.

"Thanks, Katie." Mom put the portfolio down and hugged me back.

"Well?" asked Grandmother the second we got upstairs. "Did you get the job?"

"They'll let me know. But I doubt it," said Mom.

Grandmother shook her head. "I told you not to wear that old skirt." And she gave Mom a long speech about wearing the "right" kind of clothes.

Later, when I was in bed, Mom came in. That was our just-us-two time.

I asked her, "How come Grandmother talks to you like you're still a kid?"

Mom said, "I wish I knew. Maybe she thinks there's still a chance to talk me into being more like her."

"No, please!" I put my arms around her neck. "I'm glad you're you. Mom, you know what I wish?"

"That we had a place of our own. You've told me a bunch of times."

"Yes, but I wasn't going to say that."

"What, then?"

"Oh, Mom—I saw this girl on Rollerblades, and it

looked like so much fun! Do you think I could get Rollerblades?"

"Your grandmother wouldn't like it."

"I know. But she's not my mother. And if *you* said yes—"

"They're expensive," said Mom. She looked really down. I was sorry I even asked.

So then I asked her something I figured she *could* say yes to: "Tomorrow, if you're not busy, can we do things together? Have lunch at Pizza Plenty? Explore the neighborhood?"

"You bet." And she kissed me good night.

LUZ

BUT FIRST THING next morning, somebody from *Bright Lights* magazine called Mom on the phone. There was a job in their art department. Could Mom come for an interview?

"Sure," she said. She got dressed and rushed out.

I went down with her in the elevator, just for the ride.

"Bye, Mom."

"Bye, Katie. I'll be back as quick as I can."

She looked so sorry about leaving me with nothing much to do, and nobody to do it with, that I walked her as far as the corner. Then we said good-bye all over again. And I wished her luck.

Pony let me back inside the building.

"How's it going, Katie? Want to see today's paper?"

"Yes."

He handed it to me. "Sit down. Stay awhile."

If he ever gets tired of being a doorman, maybe he could work as a mind reader. He somehow knew without my telling him that I was in no hurry to go upstairs to Grandmother.

I turned to the jobs section.

"Aren't you kind of young to be looking for a job?" he asked. His voice was so serious I burst out laughing. It felt good. It was my first real laugh since we moved here.

I said, "I'm looking for jobs for my mom. She's an artist." I started to tell him all the things she can do: design, draw, paint, lay out pages, make collages—

"*Momentito*—" All of a sudden Pony dashed outside.

Hey! I hoped the intercom wouldn't buzz and that nobody would try to get into the building. Because what was I supposed to do?

The intercom stayed quiet. Nobody tried to get in.

But then someone stepped out of the elevator—Mr. Coleman.

Mr. Coleman is old. His head is shiny and almost all bald. He has a round belly that sticks out. And he looks like he thinks he is very important.

"He *is* important," Grandmother told me once. "He is chairman of the board of managers."

She's on that board herself, along with other people who live in the building. They make rules against things. Like: no dogs; no loud noises; no ball playing outside; no Rollerblades in the lobby. Oh, and the rule that the doorman must never leave his post.

"Hi, Mr. Coleman," I said.

"Hello, er . . ." He didn't remember my name. "And where, may I ask, is Felipe?"

"He'll be right back."

Mr. Coleman frowned and shook his head. "This won't do. It won't do at all." He took loud, angry steps to the door. And he made a big deal about having to open it himself.

About a minute after Mr. Coleman stormed out, Pony came back with a kid on Rollerblades—the girl I saw yesterday!

He could only bring her as far as the door. Not inside, on account of the skates.

He motioned for me to come over.

"Katie, I'd like you to meet Luz Mendes. Luz, meet Katie Curtis. Katie's new here."

Luz—I never heard that name before. It sounded like when you're *losing*—a game or a bet or something. Funny, because I felt like I was *winning*, finally getting to meet a kid my age around here.

She was a little taller and skinnier than me. She looked full of get-up-and-go in her bright orange shorts and her matching shirt with a picture of gerbils on it. Her brown curly hair was like a light, puffy cloud around her face. Her eyes were the same color brown as her hair, with lots of sparkle in them.

We stuck our hands out. We shook.

"Nice to meet you!" we said at the same time.

Then we laughed and linked our pinkies together like you're supposed to do when that happens.

"Want to skate?" she asked.

"That would be great! Except I don't have Rollerblades."

"You don't?" She was amazed. She crinkled her eyebrows together like she was really thinking.

"What's your shoe size?" she asked finally.

"Four. Maybe four and a half by now. My feet grow so fast, I'm not sure."

"Hm. That might work." And she asked me to come over to her house. She lives in the brownstone building right next door.

"Now?" I asked.

She pulled on my hand. "Right now!"

My feet were all ready to go. I wanted to, so much! But of course I couldn't. Not just like that.

"I have to ask my grandmother."

"Want me to come with you?"

"Yes. But—" I pointed to her Rollerblades.

"I know. No Rollerblades allowed. That's okay, I'll take them off." And she did, in about one second.

We went into the lobby.

"Pony, will you watch my Rollerblades?" She put them down by the intercom.

We went up in the elevator together. It was nice, having company. But I wasn't too hopeful.

Grandmother opened the door. She looked annoyed. She was spending the morning preparing for her volunteer work, teaching English to people from other countries. And Grandmother did not like being interrupted.

"Katherine, where is your key? I thought I gave you one."

"Yes, but I forgot it. Grandmother, this is Luz Mendes. Could I—?"

"What happened to your shoes?" she asked Luz. She was staring at Luz's feet. Like wearing only socks was as bad as going around naked.

"I wasn't wearing shoes. I was blading," Luz explained.

"I see." Grandmother made a sour face and turned to me. "Katherine, what were you about to ask?"

"Um, well, this is Luz Mendes. She lives next door. She wants me to go to her house." And I asked with my best smile on, in my best voice, "Please, Grandmother, *may* I?"

"Out of the question," said the Queen of No. "I cannot let you visit people I have never met." She sounded like she meant, "And don't want to meet." Like she thought that Luz and her family weren't good enough. I hoped Luz didn't notice. I felt embarrassed, and mad.

Then I had to go inside. And Luz left. But first she wrote down her phone number, so that later my mom could call her mom and arrange for us to get together.

3 BAD DAY, GOOD NIGHT

SOME DAYS ARE a hundred hours long, and nothing good happens in any of those hours. At least that's how it felt!

Around eleven o'clock Mom called. She was stuck at *Bright Lights* magazine. They wanted her to do page layouts. It was part of the job interview, so she had to. And it would take a long time.

I finished the book I was reading, *Desert Island*. But it didn't end the way I hoped it would. I worked a two-hundred-piece puzzle. But right in the middle a big chunk was missing. I watched TV, but there was nothing good on.

Then I curled up on the window seat in the living room and looked out the window.

Grandmother came to check on me.

"Don't you have anything to do?" she asked, like that was some kind of crime.

Actually, I was busy doing two things: (1) keeping track of pigeons that flew by, and (2) telling pigeon stories to Maizie.

Maizie is not a regular-size doll, the kind that little kids play with. She's left over from a dollhouse I used to have. I think it's okay for kids my age to still have dollhouse dolls. And besides, you can always slip them in your pocket, quick, if anyone is looking.

Anyway, pigeons and Maizie were my private business, and I did not want to tell Grandmother anything about them.

So I answered, "No, I don't have anything to do." And I asked her again, just for the heck of it, "Please, may I go to Luz's house?"

Grandmother acted like she didn't even hear that. She said, "Wait. I have something for you."

She brought me a pack of crayons. And guess what else: a coloring book!

I thanked her politely. But what did she think? That I was five years old or something?

A few hundred more pigeons flew by. I got tired of thinking up stories about them. So then I really just did nothing till almost six o'clock, when Mom got back—at last!

"Mom, guess what?" I said as soon as she got in the door. "I met this girl. Her name is Luz. She's really nice. She invited me over. Grandmother didn't let me go. But can I, tomorrow? Please, please call Luz's mother. Will you, Mom?" I handed her the piece of paper with the phone number on it. I even handed her the phone.

But Grandmother was rattling pot lids, starting dinner. And Mom said, "I'd better go help her."

So we went into the kitchen. Mom took stuff for salad out of the refrigerator. And she asked Grandmother why she didn't want me to go to Luz's house.

"Well, Susan," said Grandmother in a snooty voice, "are they our kind of people?"

That made everything I'd been feeling boil up inside of me and explode. "My mother is a grown-up!" I yelled really loud. "Don't tell her what friends I can have!"

Grandmother stayed icy calm.

"Susan, don't let your daughter speak to me in that tone," she said as though I wasn't even there. And she stalked out of the kitchen.

Slam the door! I thought. Go on, bang it hard! Act mad, and get it over with!

But that's not how she is. She closed the door tight without making any noise at all.

I started to set the table. And I apologized.

"I'm sorry, Mom. I shouldn't have yelled. But please let me go to Luz's tomorrow."

Mom said to let her think about it.

When dinner was ready, she made me go knock on Grandmother's door and tell her.

Grandmother said, "I'm not hungry." So Mom and I ate by ourselves.

Afterward Mom went into Grandmother's study. "We need to talk," she said.

They "talked," all right. On and on and on.

I went into my room and played tapes. But I could still hear. Not what they said. Just their voices, arguing and fighting till long past my bedtime.

Mom looked really beat when she finally came in to say good night. So I didn't bug her again about going to Luz's house.

I was sure I wouldn't fall asleep for ages and that I was in for a long, awful night.

But just the opposite happened. I fell right asleep. And I had a great time in my dream.

I dreamed I was out in the night. The moon shone. The sidewalk glittered. I whizzed down it all the way to the end of Sycamore Street. I zoomed straight into the park that I'm never allowed to go in by myself.

I glided through the park to the river, then down along the riverbank for miles and miles. And I never even got tired! I was on Rollerblades, of course. They were like natural add-ons to my feet. I skated like I was born wearing Rollerblades and had been blading all my life.

4 ROLLERBLADES!

NEXT MORNING WHEN I woke up, I heard Mom whistling. She only whistles when she's in a good mood. That told me Grandmother was out already. And it was true. This was the day she did her volunteer work.

At breakfast Mom gave me even better news: "I called up Mrs. Mendes. It's fine with her. You can go see Luz."

I jumped up so fast I knocked over my chair.

Mom laughed. "Finish your bagel."

"I'll eat it on the way." I gave her a hug. "Thanks, Mom!"

Mom said, "Be back at twelve."

"How come?"

"So we can go to Pizza Plenty. You still want to, don't you?"

"Yes! Bye, Mom, see you then!"

I dashed to the building next door. I pressed the buzzer marked MENDES, 4C. The next second they buzzed me in, like they were waiting for me.

I ran up the three flights of stairs.

The door to 4C was open. Luz stood there.

"Hi, Katie. Look!" She held out a pair of Rollerblades.

- -

She said, "These are my brother's. But they're too small for him. Want to see if they fit?"

I shucked off my sneakers and stuck my feet in the boots.

"I think they're a little big."

"That's better than too small." Luz ran and got two pairs of socks. "Here, put these on."

I did. Now the boots fit fine.

I tried to stand up in them. That was not so easy.

I was struggling not to topple over when Luz's mom came out of their bathroom and said, "Hello. You must be Katie."

She had on white shoes and a nurse's uniform. She looked a lot like Luz, except grown up.

"Luz, did you ask Lorenzo?" she asked.

"Yes, Mami. He said he's outgrown them."

"Well, be sure you give Katie the rest of the gear. As a loan. When Lorenzo gets new Rollerblades, he'll want it back. Make sure Katie wears it all. That goes for you too, Luzita."

Mrs. Mendes pinned on her hospital ID badge and grabbed her pocketbook. "Now I have to leave or I'll be late for work. Have fun, girls. Papi's on the roof if you need anything. Bye." She rushed out.

"What's 'the rest of the gear'?" I asked.

Helmet, knee pads, elbow pads, wrist guards. Luz had hers on in two seconds. It took me a lot longer.

"You'll get used to it," Luz said. "You can start right

here in this hall. It's nice and long. Ready? Hold on to me. That way you'll be steady. Now watch what I do."

She pointed her feet out. I did, too.

She walked like that.

"Now you walk. Like a duck."

I did.

"Good. Now faster. Bend your knees. Lean forward, like this. Okay?"

"Yeah—" But my left foot started sliding out from under me, and then my right foot—"Hey! How do I stop?"

I threw myself at the wall and glommed on.

Luz laughed. "You use your brake! It's on the back of your right skate." She showed me how to use it.

Then she made me duckwalk halfway down the hall, brake, then duckwalk to the other end and back.

"When do I get to really skate instead of duckwalk?"

"Now! Watch: Point one skate out and push to the side. Now push back a little. Now shift your weight. Now push with the other skate—"

Huh? I got confused trying to do all that. So I made believe I was ice-skating, which I learned two years ago. I kind of balanced myself with my arms. And it worked.

"Hey, look! I'm doing it!"

"Great," said Luz. "You're ready for the big time. Wait for me a sec. Take your Rollerblades off."

She took hers off and ran out the apartment door,

into the landing, and up some stairs. "Papi," she called, "me and my friend are going outside. Look down and watch us skate!"

We walked in our socks down the three flights of stairs and down the stoop steps. Then we put our Rollerblades back on.

And we skated. Luz held on to me till I got steady. Then she made herself skate very slowly so we could stay side by side.

We made it halfway up to Emerson Street. We actually made it halfway up the block without me falling even once!

"You're a natural," said Luz. "When I first learned, I fell a bunch of times."

As soon as she said that, whoops, I fell, smack on my knees. But it didn't hurt because of my knee pads. I just picked myself up.

"Can you make it to the corner?" asked Luz. "There's something I want you to see."

We skated up to the traffic light at Emerson and crossed to the other side of Sycamore.

"See that?" Luz pointed to a fence with a door in it. On the door was a sign that said COMMUNITY PROJECT: DREAM GARDEN. Behind the fence were different kinds of flowers, fresh green grass, and new little trees.

"Can we go in there?" I asked.

Luz said, "Sure."

We went in and sat down on a bench.

"This is nice," I said.

"Yeah," said Luz. "But you should have seen it before! It was like a garbage dump, full of old junk and graffiti."

"So who had the dream to make it a garden?" I asked.

She smiled. She said, "Guess."

"*You?*" I asked. "No kidding, wow!"

So she told me how everybody thought it couldn't happen. But she wanted it to so much that she got people to help, mostly kids in the neighborhood. And they worked really hard cleaning it up to make the dream real.

When we skated back from the garden, I felt more steady on my blades and started going faster.

But suddenly this kid with a cocky grin *whooshed* at us from out of nowhere. He held his arms way out and hogged the whole sidewalk like it was his private property.

"Hey, you little girls, get out of my way!"

"That's Mike Donnelly," Luz told me. She yelled back at Mike, "Who're you calling 'little'?"

And *wham!* Before we knew it, all three of us were sprawled on the ground.

But it was no big deal. We got right back up. Luz

and I skated in one direction; big-shot Mike skated in the other.

After that, no more falls.

It was daytime, sunny out. We were hot and sweaty. We only skated up and down the sidewalk of Sycamore Street. But it was like in *my* dream from the night before. Like a secret door was opening up and letting me back into it. Except in my dream I'd been by myself. So this was even better!

I wished we could skate and skate, Luz and me together, for, oh, about a hundred miles.

But we had to go back to her house so I could get ready to go to Pizza Plenty with my mom.

5 MAIZIE PLAYS THE PIANO

THE SECOND WE got back from Pizza Plenty, the phone rang.

"Hi, Katie!" It was Luz. "Did you—um—leave something at my house?"

"Yes, the Rollerblades, remember? My grandmother would have a fit if I brought them over here."

Luz said, "I know. I mean something else. Are you missing anything?"

Oh my gosh . . . I reached into my pockets—empty! No Maizie!

"Yes, I'm missing something—" And I thought, What if she thinks carrying a doll around in your pocket is dumb?

But Luz asked, "What's her name?" Like she really wanted to know.

"Maizie."

"That's a nice name. I just wanted you to know that she's okay. She's having a very nice time—"

"How come?"

"She's at a party."

"She is? Where?"

"In my apartment house. For dolls, I mean," said Luz. "Want to see it?"

"Sure!"

"Well, come on back, and I'll show it to you. It's up on my roof."

It's not just Luz's roof, of course. It belongs to everybody in the building. But her family's apartment is closest to the stairs that lead to it.

It's dark inside that staircase. When you come to the top, you go through a sort of small, heavy door. Then you have to blink because suddenly it's so bright you almost can't see for a minute.

The roof is really only five floors up. But there's nothing over it except sky. When you reach out your hand, you feel like you can almost touch the blue.

When my eyes got used to so much brightness, the first thing I saw was a big wooden box with slats. There were two gerbils inside.

"The big one is Rosemary. The other one is Ramon," said Luz. "They belonged to our class. I'm just keeping them over the summer. My papi made the cage."

The cage was roomy, with soft-looking wood shavings on the floor. And there were two exercise wheels, so the gerbils didn't need to take turns. It had a food station, drinking bottles, a mirror so they could look at themselves, and even a gerbil seesaw.

I said, "It looks more like a fancy hotel than a cage."

"Yeah. My papi's really good at building things," said Luz. She started to take Ramon out for me to pet.

But just then I saw the "apartment house." And I ran right over.

It stood near the corner under an aluminum awning that kept the rain off it.

And it was made of six big cardboard cartons. They were painted the same color chocolate brown that Luz's building is. The two cartons on the bottom were the ground floor. The two on top of those were the second floor. And the two on top of those were the third floor. Each floor was a separate apartment.

On the ground floor in the middle was a big front door. Every floor had lots of windows. Some windows even had ledges with flowerpots painted on them.

I said, "Wow. This is amazing. You could never buy anything like this in a toy store. Even if you looked in every toy store in the whole city and had scads of money."

Luz grinned and said, "Wait till you see the inside."

We went around to the back. The back had a big wooden board on a hinge. When it was open, you could reach into all the apartments. They each had living rooms, bedrooms, kitchens, even bathrooms!

The second-floor apartment had the big playroom. That's where the party was.

Three dolls sat at a table, having tea. One doll aimed a dart at a tiny bull's-eye target on a wall. Two dolls stood holding each other like they were dancing. There was a piano and a piano bench—with Maizie sitting on it.

I said, "Hey, I didn't even know Maizie could play the piano!"

"She can. She's really good," said Luz. She twirled the dancing dolls around. She made one doll at the tea table clap her hands, like for applause.

I reached in to let Maizie stand up and take a bow.

Then the dart-thrower doll's mom called up from the third-floor apartment to tell him to come home.

Pretty soon all the guest dolls except Maizie had to go home. By then I knew all their names: Estrella, Margaloo, Olga, Alonzo, Felix, Guadalupe; and I knew which dolls and families belonged in which apartments.

We played that it was suppertime for all those families. And that Estrella's family was having *arroz con frijoles*. That's rice and beans. And fried bananas for dessert.

Maizie was still at Estrella's. She wanted to stay and sleep over. So we played that her mom came to get her. But Maizie said, "Please, Mom, it's so fun here. Can I sleep over?" Her mom said, "If it's okay with Estrella's mom." And it was.

While the dolls had their sleepover, Luz fed the gerbils. And I petted Ramon. His fur felt really smooth. Then I wanted to pet Rosemary. But Luz said, "Better not. She likes to take nips out of people's fingers."

Then footsteps came up the stairs and out onto the roof—Luz's papi and my mom. Mom said hi to Luz. And she asked me, "Do you know what time it is?"

"Three-thirty? Four o'clock?" I can usually tell what

time it is without looking at any clock.

But when you're up on Luz's roof, time zips by faster than pigeons fly from one end of the sky to the other. Mom showed me her watch—five-thirty!

"Come back tomorrow, okay?" said Luz.

"Sure," I answered, and I left with my mom.

The only thing friendly about going back to Number 45 was that Pony was glad to see us and asked me if I had fun today.

"Yes, I did!" I wanted to tell him where, and to say thanks for introducing me to Luz.

But the intercom started to buzz. It made an angry noise, like the person at the other end kept saying, "Make it snappy!"

At the same time, a lady needed Pony to open the front door. She was carrying big, heavy grocery bags plus a box of shirts from the laundry. The doorman is supposed to help tenants carry stuff to the elevator.

Pony got rattled—what should he do first? "Just a minute," he said into the intercom and went to help the lady. The whole time he brought her bags and clothes to the elevator, the intercom kept buzzing long and loud.

6 SOMETHING BIG

I WENT TO Luz's three days in a row.

"Again?" Grandmother asked me every time. But at least she didn't try to stop me. That was one thing she and Mom settled in their big, long talk: Mom has final say about where I can and can't go.

The best times at Luz's were when we played on her roof.

We took care of the gerbils. Luz showed me how to hold Rosemary so she couldn't nip my hand.

We sprinkled bite-size bits of bread on the corner of the ledge. That was the pigeon-feeding station. And we called: "Pigeons, come and get it!"

My favorite thing was working on the dolls' apartment house.

We put up wallpaper. Mom gave me a big stack of her samples. Luz's papi brought us some paste that real paperhangers use. He works in a hardware store, so he can get that kind of stuff.

Cutting the samples to fit the walls was tricky. And it was hard not to smear paste all over everything. But we did a good job. Especially in Estrella's playroom.

Then we decided to make something special for

Estrella. We got the idea from how Lorenzo always drummed on tables, counters, hoods of cars, anything handy.

First we needed to find some small, round, hollowed-out things. Like cups from a doll's tea set, only without handles.

"I know! My mami's sewing kit!" Luz said.

She called her mother at work and argued her into letting us borrow some thimbles.

We picked out the three shiniest thimbles. Then we cut circles out of wax paper. We glued the circles onto the thimbles. It was even trickier than putting up wallpaper.

We made sure the wax-paper circles stayed on very tight. As tight as drums. Because that's what we were making—drums! We glued two tiny cotton balls on toothpicks for drumsticks. There, all set.

Now Estrella could be a musician, too. And she and Maizie could play music together: Maizie at the piano, Estrella on the drums.

When Luz and I weren't doing things up on the roof, we were down on the sidewalk skating.

I learned to stop without bumping all over the place. I started doing turns. And I even tried skating backward.

"You're getting good," said Luz.

Yes, maybe. But she was a champ!

Luz could go full-blast fast, jump over cracks in the sidewalk, and stop on a dime. She could skate in circles. She could go down almost all the steps of the stoop without holding the rail.

"Wow, you could be in the Olympics," I said.

Luz laughed. "They don't even have blading in Olympics."

Then she said, "Wait a second—" And she got that look she gets when she's thinking up something big.

"I know," she finally said. "We could have our own Olympics Blade-a-thon!"

"Great idea!" I shouted.

We sat down on her stoop and started planning right away.

"When should it be?" I asked.

"Right now," said Luz. "I can't wait!"

But we needed time to get ready. So we decided on a week from Sunday. At ten in the morning, before it got too hot.

"And where's the best place? I know," said Luz. "This sidewalk! It's the best in the whole neighborhood for skating. And let's give out prizes in the Dream Garden."

I said, "Yes, but on the other side of the street. Or people in Number 45 will get upset and make a fuss. Like my grandmother, for instance."

We thought of all kinds of events: turning and jumping contests, regular races, relay races.

"How about skating down stoop steps?" Luz asked.

I said, "Too hard. Not many kids can do that."

While we were making all these great plans, I looked down at her brother's skates on my feet. I asked, "Won't Lorenzo feel left out?"

Luz nodded. "Yeah, he might. Except, you know what? He can be the announcer. He can borrow a boom box and be in charge of music."

I said, "That would be great."

We skated around and told all the kids we ran into. Then we made a bunch of signs. We put them up on telephone poles and on the trunk of the tree down near the end of the street:

BLADE-A-THON
SUNDAY, AUGUST 23, 10 A.M.
CORNER OF SYCAMORE AND EMERSON
IF YOU ARE BETWEEN 8 AND 12
AND HAVE ROLLERBLADES,
SIGN UP!!!

7 PICKING ON PONY

WHEN I GOT back to Number 45, I told Pony all about the Blade-a-thon.

"Cool!" he said. He really thought it was a great idea.

"Do you have Rollerblades?" I asked him.

"You bet." He got on his tiptoes, pretending they were skates, and spun around.

I said, "I bet you're a good skater. I wish you could be in the Blade-a-thon. But it's just for kids. Will you be around that day? Maybe you could be a judge or something."

Pony said, "All right! I'm off that day. But I'll come anyway. I'll watch and cheer."

I went upstairs all happy and excited.

But when I got there, Grandmother glared at me. She was acting all nervous, pushing chairs from the dining room to the living room.

"You look a sight!" she said. "Go take a shower. Be sure to scrub those knees and elbows. Put on clean clothes. Something prettier than shorts and a T-shirt, please. And hurry. I'm hosting a meeting here. People will be coming in just a short while."

"That's okay. I can stay in my room. That way they won't have to see me," I said.

"No, no. I want them to see you. I would like you to help pass the refreshments. Go on now, make yourself presentable."

So I jumped in the shower and got cleaned up. I even wore a dress and put barrettes in my hair.

The board of managers was meeting to talk about how things were going in the building. These are the people who came: Mrs. Geiger from 10A; Mr. and Mrs. Benedek from 3C; Ms. Dornberg from 9E; Mr. Aikman from the penthouse; Mrs. Zimmers from 6B; and the chairman, Mr. Coleman, from 7G.

The men wore jackets and ties even though it was a hot day. The women wore business-type suits or dresses. They all sat up very straight in their chairs.

They hardly ate any of the cookies, pretzels, or different kinds of nuts I passed around. They were too busy thinking up things to criticize. For instance:

The handymen should make less noise when collecting garbage.

The wood panels and brass in the elevators should be polished more often.

The doormen should be required to tell nannies and kids not to congregate (that means hang out) in the lobby.

Grandmother was secretary of the board. She wrote down the "minutes." "Minutes" are what everybody said.

"Oh, and speaking of doormen," said Mr. Coleman, "I'm afraid I have serious complaints about Felipe. For one thing, that ponytail of his is quite unseemly. More important, his attitude is often lax. In fact, the other day, I personally witnessed Felipe abandoning his post, leaving the door *and* the intercom unattended!"

I watched Mr. Coleman give quick little smiles after each complaint. This is his idea of fun, I thought.

"Ahem!" He gave a big loud rasp and pointed his finger at me. "Katherine is my witness. She was there when Felipe absented himself. Katherine, is that not so?"

I didn't say anything.

"Katherine, kindly answer when you are spoken to," Grandmother commanded.

So I said, "Po—I mean, Felipe—was only gone for one second."

Then I stuffed a bunch of peanuts in my mouth. It was either that or say, "Hey, cut it out! Be glad Pony works here. He's a great guy!"

All the members of the board agreed with Mr. Coleman about Pony's "attitude." I got fed up hearing about it.

"May I be excused?" I asked.

And I escaped to my room.

8 THE BLADE-A-THON

LUZ AND I were busy every second all next week, getting ready for the big day. We collected thirty empty soda bottles to use as markers in the slalom race. Plastic, of course. We made ribbon prizes to pin on the winners. And we practiced our skating. A lot. But even with all those things to do, the week felt extra long.

Finally, finally, Sunday came. And to make up for making us wait, it was nice and sunny, not too hot, and not a cloud in the sky!

I brushed my hair to make it extra shiny. Mom trimmed my bangs so they wouldn't get in my eyes. I wore my new green shorts and my shirt with the robin on it for luck. Because robins are fast flyers.

When I got downstairs at nine, Luz was already there with her Rollerblades on. She looked as sparkly as the weather in her bright blue running shorts and white shirt with sequins. Her hair was in a topknot with a silver ribbon around it.

We opened our mouths at the same moment and out came, "You look great!"

So then we laughed and linked pinkies just like that other time when we didn't even know each other yet.

"It's lucky when that happens," Luz said. "It means today will be fantastic. Don't you think so, Katie?"

I said, "Yes, yes, yes!"

But we still had a lot to do.

We rushed up to the corner of Sycamore and Emerson and crossed to the other side.

"Did you bring the chalk?" Luz asked.

"Yes, all different colors."

We squatted down and wrote START on the sidewalk in giant green, blue, yellow, red, and white letters.

"This whole sidewalk from here to the park end of Sycamore will be the Blade-a-thon raceway," said Luz. We went down there and wrote FINISH.

Then Lorenzo and their papi came over. They brought the boom box Lorenzo borrowed from a neighbor. Also a bridge table and chair.

"Good," said Luz. "That way Pony gets to sit while he's judging."

I said, "Uh-oh, I forgot to tell you. Pony can't make it. Max called in sick. He's the Sunday doorman. So Pony has to be on duty even though it's his day off."

I asked Mr. Mendes, "Could you be the judge?"

He said, "It would be an honor. But the hardware store is open Sundays, and I have to work."

"I'll do it," said Lorenzo. "I've got a stopwatch. I know all about blading. And I'll be fair."

"But you're already the DJ and announcer," Luz said.

Lorenzo said, "I can do all those things, easy."

And we said, "Okay."

Soon Mr. Mendes had to go. "So long, Luzita, Katie. *Buena suerte*." That's Spanish for "good luck."

Then Luz, Lorenzo, and I set up the soda bottles to make a curvy path all down the sidewalk for the slalom race.

We weren't even done yet when Melinda Park arrived.

"Am I early?" she asked in a shy voice.

Right after her came DeVonn Chapman, shouting "Hi!" And behind him, Shrimp Pazzalini.

"Is the first race the slalom?" asked DeVonn and swiveled his hips to get in shape.

Shrimp said, "I hope I can do this."

Peter Boyd came in his wheelchair. He was the starter.

Then a bunch of older kids showed up. Also some really little ones who could hardly skate. We had to tell them "Sorry" because of the age rule.

Finally, Mike Donnelly, Zack Wolfe, Erin Nolan, and Angela Bardos came. They were all the right ages.

"Hey, guys, when do we start? I can't wait!" Zack said.

And Mike bragged, "I'm all set to win!"

The church bell over on Palmer Street started ringing.

"Ten o'clock," said Erin. "Let's go!"

Lorenzo used his hands for a megaphone and shouted, "THE FIRST BLADE-A-THON EVENT WILL BE THE SLALOM RACE!" And he ran down to the finish line to be timekeeper.

Kids lined up at the start. Not me, because I still couldn't skate in curves that well. Luz was first in line because this whole thing was her idea.

For once no cars went by. Everything was totally quiet. Everybody waited for Peter to give the signal.

He cleared his throat. "On your mark. Get set—"

I looked at Luz. She stood as still as a thing with a spring in it, all coiled up, ready to release. She looked back at me. I think she knew what I was wishing for her: ¡Buena suerte!

"GO!" Peter yelled.

Luz took off slowly. You have to, for slalom. She cleared the first bottle in a graceful arc. Then she picked up speed. By the time she cleared the fifth bottle, she was whizzing around like curved lightning. But she was careful, too. If you knock any over, you're out.

I rooted for her so hard my insides got tied in knots.

She cleared twenty-nine bottles and made it look easy, nothing to it. Only one more bottle to go—

"Yea, Luz!" I cheered at the top of my lungs.

Ka-boom! Of course no plastic bottle could ever make that much noise falling down. But that's how loud it sounded inside my head when Luz bumped into the last one and it hit the ground.

Kids groaned, "Oh, no! Too bad!"

All except Mike. The big grin on his face said, Watch me win!

"Luz would have finished in three minutes, five seconds. Very, very fast!" Lorenzo announced really proudly and shook her hand.

DeVonn was up next. Then Shrimp.

"Three minutes, twelve seconds! Three minutes, twenty-one seconds!" Lorenzo announced their times.

The next four kids all knocked bottles over. Mike slammed into one right near the start.

Only one contestant was left: Melinda Park.

"On your mark," Peter called. "Get set, go!"

Melinda took off and cleared all thirty bottles.

"The winner! Three minutes, six seconds!" Lorenzo announced.

We all rushed down to her and cheered. Even Mike.

Melinda blushed bright red. She said "Thanks" so quietly you almost couldn't hear. But she was really, really happy, you could tell.

The next event was the smiley-face race.

Luz and I were captains and picked teams. Just for a change, the first kid I picked was Shrimp. And for another change, Mike Donnelly—the big shot—ended up getting picked last.

Captains went first. Luz and I grabbed pieces of chalk and took off at the sound of "Go!"

When we reached the finish we had to draw a smiley face on the ground. Then we raced back and handed the chalk to the next kid on the team.

Luz beat me by a lot. I knew she would. Even so, I thought my team might still win. Melinda and Erin were on it, and they were really fast.

But Luz's team won. Sure, I minded. But I was still glad for her.

"THE NEXT CONTEST IS JUMPING OVER CRACKS IN THE SIDEWALK!" Lorenzo announced.

He put a bouncy salsa tape on the boom box. Then he scurried all over the place, judging which jumps were the best.

Definitely not mine. I was still too scared of falling on my face. But the music got me in the mood, and after each jump I got a little braver.

DeVonn was in front of me. He jumped so high he looked like he was made of rubber. I almost expected him to spread his arms out like wings and fly the rest of the way.

Hey! Suddenly all the bounce went out of him. He lurched over to the nearest building. He leaned against the wall and looked at his right skate.

Lorenzo called, "Time out!"

That was when Pony came by.

I ran to him. "Hi, Pony! Don't you have to work after all? Can you stay?"

Pony said, "I'm on my break. I can stay ten minutes. What happened, DeVonn? What's wrong with your skate?"

"Beats me. It got all wobbly." DeVonn held it up.

Pony looked at it. He spun the wheels. "This front wheel got loose."

"Just my luck," said DeVonn. "Guess I'm through."

"No reason why," said Pony. "Wait. I can fix this for you in no time." He sprinted up the block and disappeared around the corner.

There's no such thing as "no time." Anything you do takes *some* time, even if you do it super fast.

Pony came back in seven minutes. I checked the time on Lorenzo's stopwatch. He brought a special wrench he'd borrowed from the hardware store.

It took him another four minutes to fix DeVonn's right front wheel.

That made a total of eleven minutes.

I remembered the board members giving all their complaints, and I got pretty worried. I said, "Pony, you'd better go back."

He said, "Nah. Nelson appreciates that I'm filling in for Max." Nelson is the super at Number 45. "He won't mind if I take an extra little while. I want to stay and watch the jumping contest."

I said, "What if Mr. Coleman or somebody on the board of managers calls on the intercom or something?"

- -

Pony stuck out his stomach so it looked like Mr. Coleman's potbelly. He made an extra-serious face and said, "He'll just have to wait."

The jumping contest started over. DeVonn's leaps were something to see.

"DeVonn is the winner!" Lorenzo shouted.

At the prize ceremony in the garden, Luz pinned ribbons on all the winners. There were lots of ribbon prizes left at the end. She picked a gold one up from the table.

"Who's it for?" I asked.

"You." She pinned it on me.

"How come?" I asked.

"Because you're a good learner. You learned really fast." She took hold of both my hands, and we whirled around in a circle. "Because it's great being friends with you. That's how come!"

9 WINNING AND LOSING

I DIDN'T WIN any race. I didn't even come close. So what? I felt like the biggest winner of the day when Luz said what she said about being friends.

Then I changed into my shoes, even though the Blade-a-thon wasn't over.

"How come?" asked Luz.

"I have to go to the bathroom."

My other reason was Pony. He stood around talking as if he had lots of time. Well, he didn't! He'd be in big trouble if he stayed away any longer.

I pulled on his sleeve. "Pony, I have to go back. Come with me? If you do, I can cross right here instead of going up to the light." I told him why I was in a hurry. It was embarrassing. But it was one way to get him to hurry, too.

Across the street at Number 45, everything was happening at once. A man with a shopping cart loaded with grocery bags needed help getting into the building. A lady needed help pushing a stroller with a baby in it out the door. And all this time the intercom was buzzing like crazy. Somebody upstairs sure wanted to tell the doorman something!

Nelson, the super, didn't know what to do first: help the man with the cart, the lady with the stroller, answer the buzz, or explain to Mr. Coleman why Pony wasn't there.

Because of course Mr. Coleman *was* there. He tap-tapped his foot on the marble floor and squinted at his watch.

When he saw us coming, he put on a phony smile and said in a phony-friendly voice, "Welcome back, Felipe. How good of you to favor us with your presence. Are you quite, *quite* certain that you are ready to resume your post?"

"Yes, sir, Mr. Coleman," said Pony. He helped the lady with the stroller out the door, and the man with the shopping cart in.

When Pony was done, Mr. Coleman gave him a big bawling out: "Young man, this is not the first time you have been tardy coming back from your break. More than merely tardy. Fifteen minutes late! I'm telling you right now, with Nelson as my witness, this simply will not do. If you value your position, you will have to pull up your socks. Do I make myself clear?"

"Very clear," Pony said. He bent down and carefully pulled his socks up: first the left one, then the right.

Mr. Coleman got so mad, he turned red from the tip of his chin to the top of his head. "Are you making fun of me? If so, you can bid your job farewell."

I saw the grin on Pony's face. And I got sad. I could

already feel the empty feeling of coming into this building without Pony there.

Don't let this happen, I thought. And I concentrated really hard on sending him an ESP message: *Pony, watch out!*

But it didn't work.

Pony straightened up.

He came over to where I was waiting for the elevator. He tipped up my face. "So long, Katie. Nice knowing you. Maybe I'll see you around." And he gave me a wonderful smile, nothing phony about it.

Then he turned back to Mr. Coleman. He put his hand to his forehead in a kind of salute.

"I quit," he said, loud and clear. And he marched out the door.

10 BREAKING THE RULE

THERE ARE TWO kinds of grown-ups in the world: the ones who talk to kids as if what we think matters, and the ones who don't.

The new doorman, Otto, was the second kind. He didn't even bother asking kids "How are you?" Only grown-ups. Because grown-ups give tips. Kids don't.

I kept hoping I'd see Pony around. I didn't.

But Luz did. He was friendly with her family and went there to visit sometimes. She told me he was looking for another job. He was pretty sure he'd find one soon.

I already envied the kids in the building where he'd work. That's how much I missed talking to him.

About two weeks after Pony quit, Luz and I were up on the roof. We and the gerbils, Rosemary and Ramon, were the audience at a concert at the dolls' apartment building.

For a change Estrella was playing the piano. And Maizie sat at the drums.

Bang, bang, bang. I kept hearing this noise. First I pretended it was Maizie beating out a rhythm.

It got louder and louder.

Luz asked, "What's doing that? Where's it coming from?"

Not from the street. Or the alley in back. Not the brownstone on the left. It was coming from the building on the right, Number 45.

We listened hard.

"It's coming from higher than our roof," said Luz.

We looked up along the side wall at all the windows.

The banging kept on.

"Hey, Luz, I see something!"

"What? Where, Katie?"

"That window on the seventh floor—"

"What about it?"

It was the frosted kind that bathrooms have: the kind you can't see through.

I said, "Take a good look. Can you see a shape behind it? A big, round shape? Watch—"

"Yes! Moving back and forth! Is that what's banging on the window—"

Suddenly the window flew open. The shape leaned out. Its head was wrapped up in a towel. It was a person, a man, screaming at the top of his lungs, "HELP! I'M STUCK! I CAN'T OPEN THE DOOR! SOME-BODY, GET ME OUT OF HERE!!!"

Luz and I got the giggles. Well, really, the giggles got us. We giggled so much we thought we'd never stop.

When I finally caught my breath, I said, "Do you know who that is?"

"Ursula the witch from *The Little Mermaid*? That's who it looks like with that white towel thing on," Luz said.

"Well, it isn't. It's Mr. Coleman."

Luz didn't know who that was.

So I told her. "He's practically the boss of the whole building. He's the one who had it in for Pony. He got Pony so upset he had to quit."

"Sounds like a mean guy," said Luz. "But we have to do something to get him out of there."

Yes, right.

We yelled across to Mr. Coleman, "Don't worry! We'll get someone to get you out." We tried waving our arms like windmills so he'd notice us. But he was still banging and screaming so loud he didn't see or hear us.

We ran downstairs and headed next door.

I said, "Nelson has keys to all the apartments. We'll just tell the doorman, and he'll tell Nelson, and Nelson will take care of it."

The new guy, Otto, was on duty. When I saw his stony face, I hung back.

"Come on." Luz pulled at me.

"No, wait. Listen, Luz, wouldn't it be great if—"

"If what?" she asked.

"If Pony could be the one to go rescue Mr. Coleman?"

One great thing about Luz is how fast she catches on.

"Yeah!" she said, and her eyes lit up. "I know where he is. I *think* he's there, anyway."

"Where?"

"At a volleyball game. He said there was going to be one today. And that he hoped to play in it. He wasn't sure he could. But he said he'd try—"

"In the park, you mean? We're not allowed to go in there alone—"

"I know," said Luz.

We looked in each other's eyes. One thing about friends is sometimes you know what the other is thinking, just like that. Because it's what you're thinking, too.

We took each other's hands and zipped down to the end of Sycamore Street. We looked both ways, even though cars almost never go there. We crossed Park Road, passed the statue of General Ulysses S. Grant on horseback, and went inside the park.

Luz said, "I sure hope Pony's there. Or we could get in trouble for nothing."

Yeah. I sure hoped so, too.

11

TO THE RESCUE

THE PARK IS nice. It has tall trees that give shade. It has lawns and benches. But people leave trash around. And some places in the park are scary. Like, for instance, the tunnel that leads to the volleyball field. Homeless people keep their stuff in there.

I clutched Luz's hand. She clutched mine. We ran into the tunnel.

A shape wearing a stocking cap lay curled up by the wall. We ran past on tiptoe. But the person woke up. It was a woman. She shook her fist at us and screeched, "Brats, get outta here!"

When we got to the volleyball field, eight men were playing. But not Pony.

One man sat on the grass, watching the game.

"That's our next-door neighbor, Mr. Diaz," said Luz.

Mr. Diaz yelled to us, "You girls shouldn't come in the park by yourselves!"

"I know. But it's an emergency. We're looking for Pony," Luz said. "We have to find him! It's really important!"

Mr. Diaz said, "You just missed him. He skinned his knee and went to Cherry's for Band-Aids."

"Thanks!" called Luz. And we started to run.

Mr. Diaz caught up with us. "I'll go with you. If it's that important, we'd better catch him, right?"

Mr. Diaz was such a fast runner we almost couldn't keep up with him. We wished we had on our Rollerblades.

We took the Alston Street park exit to Cherry's Drugstore. We got there in two minutes flat. We looked all around. No Pony.

Then suddenly someone said "Thanks" in a voice we knew.

"There he is," said Mr. Diaz. He shook a finger at Luz, but not in a mean way. "You stay out of that park, you hear?" And he left.

Pony was sitting behind the counter where people get prescriptions. The pharmacist was cleaning the scrape on his knee.

"Pony, you have to come with us!" said Luz.

"Because guess what? Mr. Coleman is stuck in his bathroom!" I said. I couldn't help it, a little giggle came out.

"I'm sorry to hear it," Pony said. He didn't sound that sorry. "But what does it have to do with me?"

"Don't you see?" asked Luz. "*You* have to get him out!"

"That's right," I said. "Because then he'll be sorry you quit."

"There." The pharmacist stuck on the Band-Aids. "That ought to do it."

Luz and I begged, "Come with us, Pony! Please? *Please?*"

Till he finally said, "Okay. But only because you're asking me so nicely."

It was just two blocks from Cherry's to Number 45 Sycamore Street. Pony's knee slowed him down, but not very much. So we got there pretty fast.

I told the new doorman, "Please get Nelson. There's an emergency."

"Oh, really?" Otto didn't budge.

"Yes, really. You'd better hop to it," said Pony. "A tenant is locked in his bathroom. These girls heard him yelling for help. Tell Nelson to bring the keys for 7G."

"7G?" This got Otto's attention. "You mean Mr. Coleman?"

"Right. I used to be doorman here. I'll mind the door while you're gone. Run!" said Pony.

Otto came back with Nelson.

"Hey, Pony, put it there!" Nelson was glad to see him. "And thank you, girls, for keeping your ears open. All right, gang. Let's go to the rescue."

Nelson, Pony, Luz, and I rode up to the seventh floor. Nelson opened the door to 7G.

We went through the entrance hall and down a corridor into the master bedroom.

"HELP! HELP! I CAN'T TAKE MUCH MORE OF THIS!" yelled Mr. Coleman from the bathroom behind the bedroom. He banged so loud and hard I thought the door would break.

It didn't. But the doorknob was off it.

Nelson called to him, "This is the super, Mr. Coleman. Take it easy. We'll get you out." And he asked, "Do you have a screwdriver?"

"Are you completely out of your mind?" Mr. Coleman sounded like he wanted to roar. But after all that yelling he didn't have too much voice left. "Why would I keep a screwdriver in my bathroom?"

"I didn't mean that, Mr. Coleman," Nelson answered. "I just meant, do you have one somewhere in your apartment?"

"How should I know?" answered Mr. Coleman. "My housekeeper keeps track of such things. Try the tool-box in the linen closet."

We looked in the toolbox. It had all kinds of tools. Just no screwdriver.

"I'll have to go downstairs and get one of mine," Nelson called.

"Why didn't you bring one in the first place?" Mr. Coleman gave the door a few more big, loud bangs. "Hurry up! Don't take all day!"

"Such a nice gentleman. And so polite," said Pony in a whisper.

"Try to calm him down," Nelson told us. And he left.

"Calm him down? He'd bust a gut if he knew I was

here," Pony whispered. He was kneeling by the door, squinting at the hole where the doorknob used to be.

Luz and I crawled around on the floor, looking for the knob.

"Hey, here it is," said Luz. "Can this get the door unstuck?"

Pony shook his head. "The knob's no good without the spindle."

"What's a spindle?" we asked. It sounded like something from *Sleeping Beauty*.

"The thin metal piece that fits inside the knob. It's about four inches long," Pony said. "If we find that, we're in business."

So then the three of us scurried around on all fours, searching all over the place. The entire time, Mr. Coleman kept banging on the door.

I scooted into the corner near the bathroom. I thought I saw something. I snatched it up. "Pony, is this it?"

Pony said, "Yes! Good for you!"

"No, good for *you*, Pony, if it'll work," I said.

And Luz said, "Hurry up, try it!"

Bang, bang, bang, went Mr. Coleman. And he shouted, "When is that slowpoke super coming back?"

With all that banging, Pony had a hard time fitting the spindle into just the right place in the door.

"It has to catch inside the lock," Pony whispered. It took him seven tries.

On the eighth try, the spindle caught. Pony began to turn the knob.

"Stand back, Mr. Coleman," Pony called—too late.

The lock gave way. Suddenly the door sprang open. *Wham!* Out fell Mr. Coleman. He'd been pushing on the door with his whole weight.

He landed on his stomach.

He looked like a giant snowball, lying there with his white terry-cloth robe bundled around him. The thick, soft carpeting kept him from hurting himself.

Pony helped him up.

"Felipe?" Mr. Coleman sounded dazed. "What are *you* doing here?"

Then he saw me and Luz. "And what are Ms. Davidson's granddaughter and that other little girl doing in my apartment?"

"Here's what happened, Mr. Coleman," Pony explained. "Katie and Luz were playing on the roof next door. It's lucky for you they heard you. Otherwise you'd still be yelling and banging. Anyway, the girls went and got me. Then Katie here found the spindle that was missing. And, well, I don't mean to claim credit, but with that spindle I was able to get the door open—"

"You *deserve* credit," Mr. Coleman interrupted. "Much credit, Felipe. I had a terrible time in there. Tell me how I can thank you."

"That's okay. I was glad to do it," Pony said.

I looked Mr. Coleman in the eyes. I concentrated with all my might, trying to signal with ESP. *The way you can thank Pony—I mean, Felipe—is to ask him if he'll come back to work as doorman.*

Mr. Coleman cleared his throat. "Ahem—"

Was he getting the message? I kept my eyes glommed onto his. And I signaled, *Go on, ask him, please, please!*

And Mr. Coleman said, "Felipe, as head of the board of managers, I would like to invite you to take back your job."

Pony stood there looking from me to Luz with his eyes shining. It was like he was saying, See what you girls made happen!

"Well?" Mr. Coleman held out his hand.

Pony took it and shook. "Yes, I think I will take my job back, Mr. Coleman. Thank you, sir."

Luz and I were so excited, we jumped up and down like two yo-yos on strings. I felt like shouting *Yea! Hurray!* So I did.

12 A PERFECT PLACE

YOU CAN'T EXPECT grown-ups to change all of a sudden. After all, it took them a long time to get the way they are. And usually they *don't* change.

Except, when Pony came back on the job, Mr. Coleman asked him, "How are you doing?" And smiled at him. And thanked him for holding the door.

And just yesterday, Mr. Coleman asked him, "How are you doing, *Pony*?"

Well, that's because something big happened to make him act different. Getting stuck in the bathroom, I mean.

But sometimes nothing that big happens. Like with my grandmother.

On Monday, Luz came over—finally! Mom invited her. I was really glad because I'd been to Luz's house about a hundred times.

Grandmother was out playing bridge. And usually when she did that she stayed out till dinnertime.

Luz, Mom, and I had the Three-Way Special from Pizza Plenty for lunch: sausage, pepperoni, and mushroom. That worked out great because Luz liked all three toppings.

- -

After lunch we spread newspaper on the dining-room table. Mom brought out her carton of supplies that she uses for collages and constructions: pipe cleaners, wire, toothpicks, glue, different kinds of paper, cardboard, Styrofoam—all kinds of stuff for making shapes and sticking them together.

We made a mailbox, a fire hydrant, an apple tree, and bushes to put around outside the dolls' apartment house.

We were starting to make flowers when I heard the front door.

Uh-oh. Grandmother.

Either we'd worked longer than we thought, or she was back early.

"She won't be thrilled about us working in here," said Mom.

Right. And I thought, She won't like that Luz is here, either.

Grandmother came in, tap, tap, on her fashionable heels, in her elegant gray suit and pearl necklace.

When she saw all the stuff spread out on the table, and some scraps on the floor, the look on her face said, This mess can't be happening. Not in *my* dining room!

"Don't worry, Mother. We'll clean it all up," said Mom.

I sat there waiting for the storm to break.

But Luz stood up and went over to her.

"Hi, Ms. Davidson," she said in her friendliest voice. "I'm Luz Mendes, Katherine's friend. You met me before, when I came up in just my socks, remember?" Then, quick, she bobbed down with one knee bent in front of her. That's a curtsy. I know the word from a book about olden times. It's something people used to do when they wanted to be extra polite.

Grandmother's face uncreased into the biggest smile I ever saw on her. And she said, "I'm very pleased to meet you again, Luz. You have charming manners." And she asked, "May I see what you made?"

She looked at the tree and the other things. "Very nice," she said. She even sounded like she meant it.

And when Luz was leaving, Grandmother said, "Come visit Katherine again soon." It was a real invitation.

Still and all, she didn't change that much. Because later, she gave Mom a big, long lecture about the dining-room table and the dining-room rug. They were valuable antiques. And what could have possessed Mom to let us work in there?

Next day, up on the roof, Luz and I set up the mailbox and other things outside the dolls' apartment house.

While we were doing that, Luz said, "Your grandmother isn't so bad."

I said, "She was okay yesterday. She liked you. But

later she went back to her old self. Whew, I can't wait till we're out of there."

Luz looked up from trying to decide where to put the apple tree.

"When will you be out of there?" she asked.

"My mom may have a job doing window displays. It's almost definite. As soon as they let her know, we'll start looking for a place of our own."

Luz let the apple tree slide to the ground. She plunked herself down next to it and groaned, "Oh, no. I don't want to go through that again!"

I asked her, "What do you mean, 'go through that again'?"

So then she told me about her friend Rosie, who used to live downstairs. They had great times. They did everything together. Then Rosie moved away to another city.

"I missed her a lot. I still do," Luz said.

"Listen, Luz. It won't be like that." I pulled her up from sitting there and over to the middle of the roof. "Look around."

"Okay, I'm looking. So?"

"So, when my mom and I move, you'll probably be able to see our building from right here. Mom already promised me: We're not moving out of this neighborhood. And I'm promising you now: We'll still live near each other. You can come over any time you want."

"And will *you* still come over any time *you* want?" Luz asked.

"You don't have to ask me that," I said. Then we went back over to the dolls' apartment house.

Luz picked up the apple tree we made. She said, "I know where this tree should go. Right near the main entrance."

We got some soil from a bag of potting soil that Luz's mom uses for her plants. We put the soil around the tree and patted it down firm.

I said, "It's perfect there."

"Yeah," Luz agreed.

A bunch of pigeons came flying past just then. We looked up into the bright sky and watched them go. A little bit of wind blew our hair around.

When we couldn't see the pigeons anymore, we tilted our heads back. We closed our eyes. We let the sun shine on our faces.

"And you know what else? It's perfect here, too," I said.

Luz nodded. "I know what you mean."